WELCOME TO

YOUR **AMAZING** adventures™

Inside awaits an adventure that only you can have. It takes place in faraway, long ago lands. Monsters, sorcerers, and evil kings may oppose you, but you have the power to outwit them all. Your skill at pathfinding can steer you through all the perils, natural and otherwise, that stand in your path. If you are a good explorer of the mazes that block your journey, you'll win through in the end.

And if you get caught in the pitfalls of a maze, you can retrace your steps and try to find a better way out. That way, your skill determines the outcome.

You can be the hero, and save the kingdom from the evil forces that threaten it.

If you're ready to go for it, turn the page and see what challenges await you.

Good luck!

YOUR AMAZING adventures™ #1

THE CASTLE OF DOOM

by
Richard Brightfield

Illustrated by Paul Abrams

TOR

A TOM DOHERTY ASSOCIATES BOOK

A Tor Book, published by arrangement with Bluejay Books Inc.
Published by Tom Doherty Associates, 8-10 W. 36th Street, New York, New York 10018

A Bluejay Books Production

First printing, December 1984

ISBN: 0-812-56036-1
CANADIAN ISBN: 0-812-56037-X

Printed in the United States of America

ATTENTION!

You are about to enter an exciting world of sword and sorcery. *You* are the hero or heroine. You will have many adventures and face many dangers, but be especially careful going through the mazes—a wrong turn may be your last.

Once you have started on a path inside a maze, DON'T GO BACK—unless you reach a dead end. Finally, you will either get through the maze or enter a trap. Turn to the page indicated to discover your fate.

You are an adventurer returning from a voyage to the islands of the Western Sea. Your small boat, its one square sail swelled before an evening breeze, cuts through the waves off the Dracan coast. You are coming up fast on the harbor of Trangor. Behind you, the last scarlet banners of the setting sun are fading away on the western horizon. You stand at the tiller, your eyes scanning the approaching waterfront. Beyond the harbor is the city with its royal palace high up on a hill in the distance. Overhead, the stars are popping out in the already deep purple sky.

A few lights sparkle along the waterfront and in the city. But somehow, it seems strangely dark—and quiet. You ease your boat up against a long pier.

"I don't like it," says Thea, your friend and partner, and the only other person on the boat. "There's something scary about the waterfront tonight. It's—"

"Too quiet," you say.

"And there's no sign of Teppin," Thea says, as she takes off a narrow-brimmed hat, letting her long, blonde hair fall loose. "Wasn't he supposed to be here to meet us?"

"That's right," you answer. "He's usually right on time. We're the ones who are a little behind schedule. But don't worry, we'll find our way to the market square and catch up with him later."

"If we can find our way through the dangerous maze of dark back streets of Trangor!" exclaims Thea.

"We'll be all right," you say, "you've got your whip and I've got my slingshot. Right now what we need is a mule or a pony with a cart to carry our bags of spices."

"I'll go find something," says Thea. "As I remember, there's a stable nearby."

"Be careful," you say. "Stay to the shadows and keep your whip handy. I'll secure the boat and unload the spices onto the pier."

Thea disappears into the night. By the light of a single lantern, you take down the sail and fold it, storing it on one side of the small cabin. Then you start carefully hauling out several large sacks.

You are finishing, when you hear the clip clop of hooves coming down the pier. As the sound gets closer, you see Thea in the dim light leading a pony—and behind the pony, a cart.

"See you were lucky," you call out.

"Lucky is right," says Thea. "The man who runs the stable was just locking his gate for the night. Funny, he was very nervous, but he wouldn't tell my why. The streets are deserted too."

You and Thea load the sacks of spices onto the cart.

"Seems like Teppin would've gotten here by now—even if he was going to be late," says Thea.

"Teppin can take care of himself," you say. "There must be a good reason why he's not here."

"I sure hope we find him at the market," says Thea.

"I don't know if we will or not," you say, "but we're all ready to go."

"Are you sure we can find our way?" asks Thea.

"Just follow me," you say. "We'll be through the city in no time.

Go to next page.

Ahead of you is the maze of the city of Trangor. Find your way from the waterfront to the market. And remember what it says on page 5.

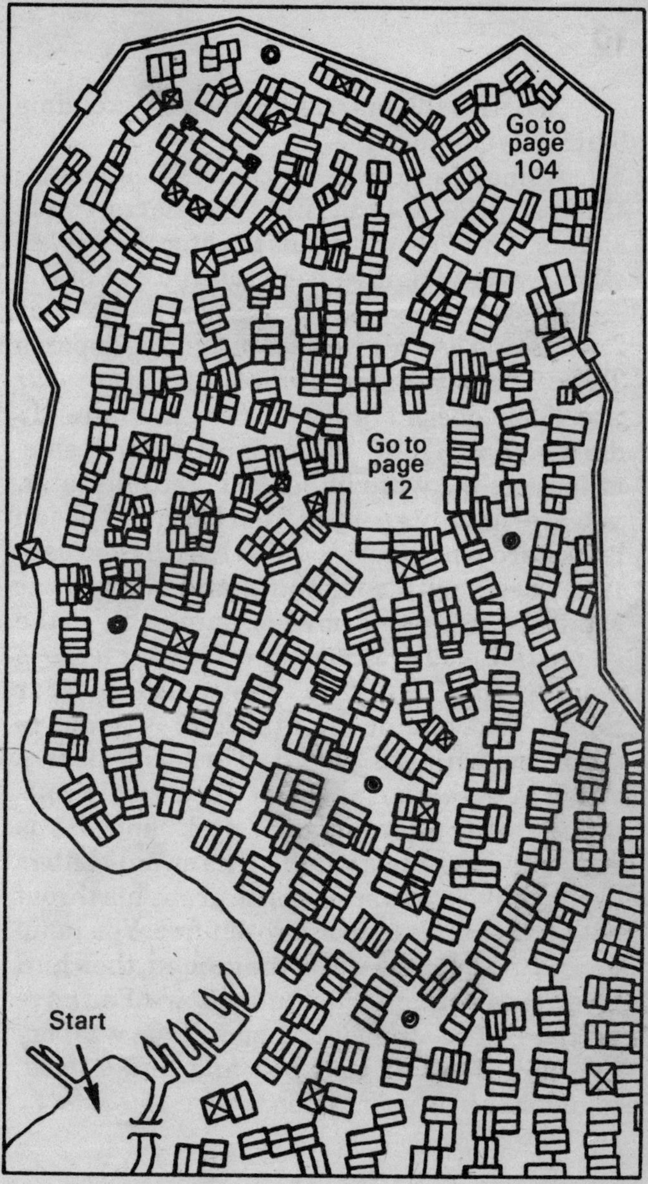
Go to page 104
Go to page 12
Start

"There's the market up ahead!" exclaims Thea. "We made it!"

A small lantern in the center of the square throws a faint light into the narrow side streets. You are just about to enter the square when several figures come at you out of the darkness.

"Looks like we're in for it," you whisper to Thea. "Let's try plan number one."

Thea doesn't answer. She has already ducked down and slipped off to the side, unloosing the whip in her belt. Seconds later, you are roughly grabbed from behind. You jab backward with your elbow as hard as you can. It connects with something and one of your attackers lets out a howl of pain. But, at the same time, you are knocked off of your feet. As you struggle to get up, you realize to your horror that one of the attackers is about to stab you with his sword. Then you hear a swish in the air as the end of Thea's whip coils around the swordsman's neck and he is suddenly jerked backwards. The sword clatters to the cobblestone street as he grabs his throat with both hands to tear himself free. You jump up and grab the sword on the ground, then hurl it as far as you can into the shadows. You have no need of it—the slingshot is your weapon. You pull it out of your belt and find a good, round stone in your pouch.

Suddenly, Thea cries out as two of the attackers grab her and start dragging her off. They are pulling her toward the square. You take careful aim with your slingshot and bounce a stone off of the head of one of them. He goes flying forward, landing with a thud on the ground. Thea catches the other one in the ankle with a sharp side kick. He lets go of her and hops around on one foot, crying in pain.

Thea runs back to see if you are all right. The two of you stand side by side—backs against a stone wall, ready for the next attack. But all you hear are footsteps fading into the distance. Faint groans come from that direction—then silence. The silence is quickly broken by the neigh of the pony nearby.

"I'd forgotten all about the pony during the fight," you say.

You go over and check the sacks in the cart. They are all OK. Then you lead the pony down the rest of the block and into the market square.

"Where is everybody?" Thea asks. "There should be at least a few traders unpacking and getting ready for the morning."

Suddenly, a line of figures appears at the far side of the square. Even in the dim light you can tell that they aren't here for the market. They're soldiers—with crossbows.

"I think we're in for more trouble,"

whispers Thea. "What's your plan this time?"

"I think we'll have to wait and see on this one," you say.

One of the soldiers—an officer—comes over to you and Thea.

"Don't you know that this market has been closed for several weeks!" he barks. "We'll have to take you to the palace until your reason for being here has been checked. We'll take care of your merchandise, traders—if that's what you are."

Go to next page.

The officer makes a gesture with his hand and several of the soldiers advance to surround you. They lead you up to the palace. There, they take you and Thea to a small room with two cots.

"You can rest here until morning," says one of the soldiers, pushing shut a heavy oak door—and locking you in.

You and Thea try to rest, but it's hard to do with the heavy tramp of feet marching past the door all night.

"I can't understand it," says Thea. "Trangor used to be such a peaceful city."

"They must be in a state of war with somebody," you say. "They probably think that we're spies."

Finally, toward morning, you and Thea manage to doze off. The sun is barely up, when the oak door swings open with a bang.

"The king himself wants to see you," says a guard at the door.

You follow the guard down a long corridor to the throne room. The king is there sitting on a high throne with advisors on both sides of him.

"So these are the two that fought off the attackers in the market district," says the king.

"And so well," says one of the advisors. "From the reports of our agents in town—"

"Yes, yes!" exclaims the king. "They

definitely could be the ones to do it."

"The ones to do what?" you ask.

"The ones to rescue my daughter," answers the king. "Some brigands have kidnapped her. They've taken her to an old castle at the far side of the kingdom. That is, I think that's what they've done."

"Most assuredly, sire," says another of the advisors. "It is the castle of the evil wizard, Kralux—often referred to as the Castle of Doom."

"Speaking of wizards!" exclaims the king. "Where is my wizard, Zinkor?"

"I'm right here, sire," says a deep, booming voice from the back of the chamber.

A tall, bearded figure strides up to the king. He is dressed in a long robe decorated with stars and moons and other astrological symbols. Behind him is a boy, dressed in a simplified version of the wizard's costume and topped with a large turban.

"Ha! Just in time! I'm about to send these two out to rescue my daughter," the king says, pointing at you.

"Just a minute!" you exclaim. "Even if we agree, what makes you think we can."

"My advisors seem to feel that you are brave, resourceful, and all that sort of thing. I do hope you'll go."

"We'll give it a try," you say, "but first we'd

like—"

"Give it a try! Give it a try!" Zinkor booms. "Do you really think that these two will last two seconds near the Castle of Doom—if they even get that far. You remember what happened to the others you sent."

"We're not afraid!" Thea speaks up.

"Bravo! Well said!" exclaims the king.

"First we need horses, provisions for the trip, and we have to find our friend Teppin," you say.

"Teppin?" asks the king. "Don't we have someone by that name down in the dungeons. It seems to me that I saw that name on some list or other."

"I believe so, sire," says one of the advisors. "He was put there for causing a disturbance in a tavern and—"

"All right! All right!" exclaims the king. "Release him at once and see to it that these two get everything they need. I want them to start as soon as possible."

"Aren't we forgetting something?" Zinkor says.

"What's that?" asks the king.

"The royal maze. You know that all new employees of the king have to go through it," Zinkor says.

"Come now," says the king, "we can dispense with that in this case."

"But sire," Zinkor continues, "if you make an exception now, your subjects will lose respect for you."

"Oh, all right," says the king. "If they have to, they have to."

"We'll be through the maze in no time," you say, "and then we'll be on our way."

"Don't be too sure of that," says Zinkor under his breath.

The guards lead you and Thea to a place deep under the palace and to the entrance to the royal maze.

Go to next page.

Find your way through the royal maze. Watch out for pitfalls, and remember what it says on page 5.

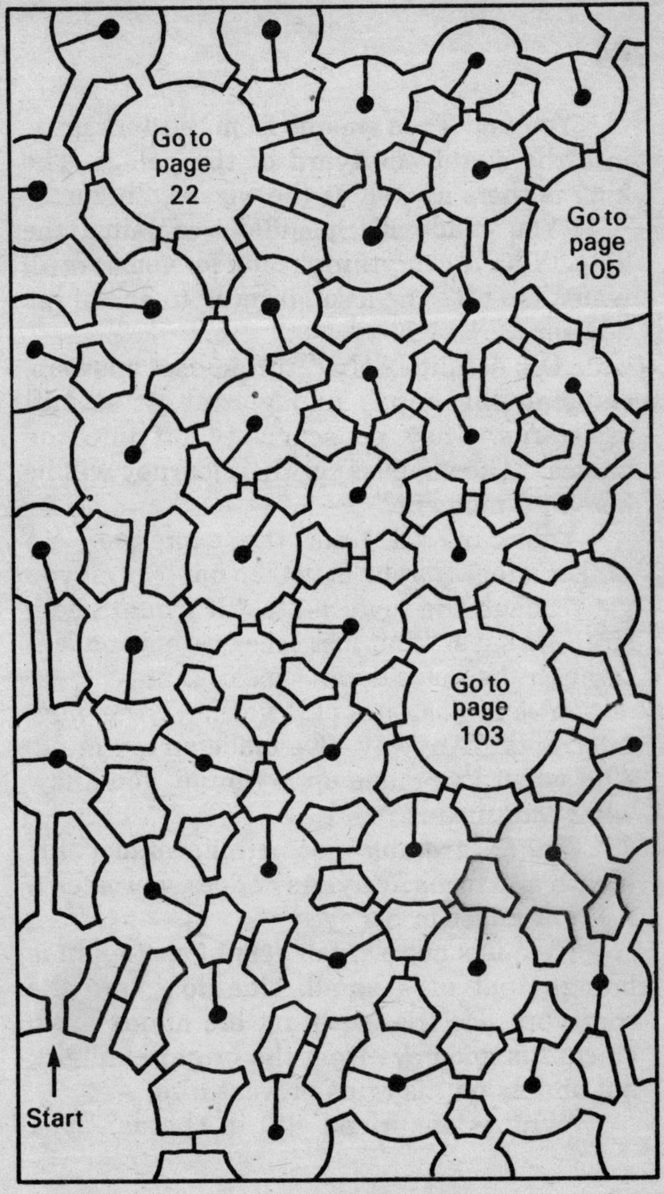
Go to page 22
Go to page 105
Go to page 103
Start

You and Thea emerge from the dark maze into the sunlit courtyard of the palace. The king is there as well as the wizard, Zinkor.

"You made it! Splendid!" exclaims the king. "I have everything ready for you. It *is* all ready, isn't it?" he asks, turning to one of his advisors.

"Oh, definitely sire!" the advisor answers, clapping his hands and glaring at several assistants. They go scurrying off into the palace. "The supplies for their journey will be here in a moment."

You can tell from the expression on Zinkor's face that he is not too happy that you got through the royal maze. "If I might add, sire," he says, "that just because they made it through the maze doesn't mean that—"

"You're just an old worrier," the king interrupts. "Anyway, I've made up my mind. And when I've made up my mind, you know what *that* means."

Zinkor grumbles something under his breath and turns away. As he does, you catch a flash of anger in his eyes.

Thea lets out a cry of delight as Teppin is brought out of a small, side door into the courtyard. He tries to bring his hands up to shield his good eye from the bright sunlight, but chains on his arms prevent him.

"Why is our friend still in chains?" you

demand.

"Yes! Why *is* this man still—" the king starts to say to an advisor.

"Just an oversight, sire," the advisor blurts out before the king has a chance to finish the question. "Remove that man's chains at once!" orders the assistant.

One of the guards runs over to Teppin, and after some effort at getting them loose, the chains clatter to the ground. Teppin stretches and rubs his good eye. The other one is covered as always by a black patch. Thea runs over and throws her arms around him.

"How could you do that to my friend!" Thea shouts, looking back accusingly at the king.

"It's all right," says Teppin. "I don't blame them. I was a bit rough with a few of the royal guardsmen in a tavern a few nights ago."

"We were worried when you didn't show up at the pier to meet us," you say, "and—"

"Enough of this talk!" the king interrupts. "Now that your friend is free, I suggest that you get going. My daughter isn't getting any younger."

"As soon as our horses and supplies get here," you say.

"Supplies and horses!" exclaims the king. "You're right. Where *are* they?"

"Here they are now!" the king's assistant cries with relief as a group of soldiers enters the courtyard leading the horses. Each horse has a saddle with a large pack behind it.

"You see! When I give an order it gets carried out. Isn't that right, Zinkor?" says the king, looking around for his wizard.

But Zinkor is gone.

"Oh well," sighs the king, "I guess that's what wizards are supposed to do—appear and disappear."

You, Thea, and Teppin climb into your saddles and start toward the palace gate.

"Some of my guardsmen will escort you as far as the Swirry River," shouts the king. "From there you're on your own. Good luck!"

You ride down the narrow streets between the palace and the east gate. Even though it's broad daylight, the streets are deserted. You catch the look on a frightened face that is cautiously looking out of a window—but it ducks out of sight as you look in that direction.

A narrow trail leads away from the city and down a steep slope. Three of the king's guards are riding some distance in front of you and three more are not far behind.

"Those guardsmen look kinda mean," you whisper to Teppin, leaning as far out of the saddle in his direction as you can. "I'm glad they're on our side."

"They may or may not be on our side," says Teppin. "We should be careful."

"What do you mean by that?" you ask. "Do you think this is a trap?"

"Well, while I was a 'guest' in the king's dungeon, I heard a lot of talk," says Teppin. "strange things are going on in this kingdom, and it's hard to tell who is on who's side."

Thea, who has been riding in front, reins back her horse until she is close enough to you and Teppin to talk.

"I don't like the way those guardsmen have been looking back at us," she says. "They put their hands on their swords every time they turn in the saddle to look at us."

"That's what Teppin and I have been talking about," you say. "We might have to make a run for it."

"But they have us boxed in," Thea says. "Half of them are in front of us and the other half behind."

"That also means," you say, "that they have their forces divided. If they try anything, we'll charge straight ahead."

"Good idea," says Teppin. "If they're going to make a move, they'll probably do it before we reach the river. Fortunately, I got my long knife back when they released me."

After riding for a couple of hours, the walls of the city have dropped out of view way behind you. The countryside is now made up of rolling hills, the sides of which are quilted with patches of fields and woods. At the top of a particularly high hill, you catch your first glimpse of the River Swirry far ahead—a silver ribbon of water glinting in the sunlight. In another hour you are descending a long slope toward a ferry station far below.

Suddenly, one of the guardsmen behind you gives a low whistle, and all of them draw their swords. Then, in a flash, they are charging you from both directions.

Go to next page.

Teppin gallops his horse straight ahead. You and Thea follow him. The guardsman in the lead raises his sword and tries to bring it down on Teppin's head. But Teppin ducks the strike and at the same time cuts the strap holding the saddle to the guardsman's horse. He goes flying off, saddle and all. Thea's whip wraps around the second guardsman, and she jerks him from the saddle. The third guardsman in front is so surprised by all of this that he pulls back too hard on the bridle, causing his horse to buck—toppling *him* to the ground.

You are past the three guardsmen in front, but the ones behind are still charging. They are almost on top of you. Suddenly, they stop short, a look of horror on each of their faces.

Go to next page.

"Wow! I wonder what made them do that," shouts Thea, taking a quick look at the guardsmen still standing frozen with fear on the road behind. "They look like they're seeing a monster or something like that."

"Whatever it is," says Teppin, "we're lucky that they stopped. We took the first three by surprise, but the others—"

Teppin stops in mid-sentence as he sees a young boy with a turban on the road ahead waving to them to stop. You and Thea recognize him immediately. It's the wizard's apprentice from the palace. You all rein your horses to a stop in front of him.

"The apparition that I set up to stop the guardsmen will last for only a short while," says the boy. "In a few seconds, it will fade and they'll be after you again, all six of them."

Go to next page.

"Then we'd better get going and fast!"

"Wait!" says the boy. "There's another way, though it can be dangerous. I can put you all into an illusion maze. To the guardsmen you will appear to vanish, but you will still have to find your way through the maze in order to escape."

"What's the dangerous part?" you ask, looking back down the road where the guardsmen are regrouping and preparing to come after you again.

"If you get lost in the maze," says the boy, "you will . . . well, let's say, be in there a long time."

"That doesn't sound *too* bad," Thea says, "at least compared to what's coming after us now."

All of you watch as the guardsmen remount their horses and come charging down the road.

"We'll try it," you, Thea, and Teppin all say at the same time.

"All right," says the boy, making some complicated gestures in the air. "I'll meet you at the other end—if you make it. Good luck!"

You start to fade just as the guardsmen reach you. You enter the maze of illusion, but you are not safe yet.

Find your way through the illusion maze—but be careful, dangers lurk in unexpected places.

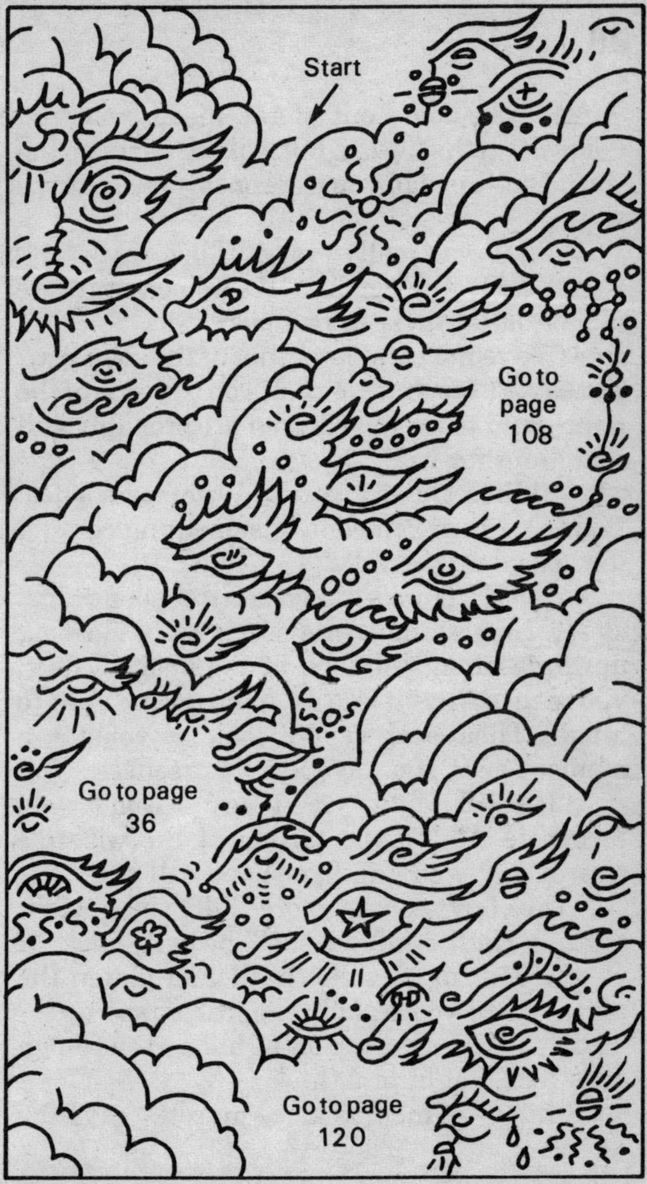
Start
Go to page 108
Go to page 36
Go to page 120

As you come out of the maze, you find yourself on the top of a hill looking down on the river. But the road you were on is nowhere to be seen.

"That was really scary," Thea says.

"Yea!" says Teppin. "We're lucky that we all got out of there in one piece."

"We're not completely out of the soup yet," you say. "I see that we're still on this side of the river—and those guardsmen are probably still searching for us."

"Shush! Quiet a second," whispers Thea. "I think I hear someone or something coming toward us up the hill."

You all crouch down as the sounds get closer. Something white seems to be floating upwards along the tops of the bushes. Then you realize what it is. You stand up and start to laugh. Thea and Teppin look at you for a moment as if you have lost your senses.

"It's all right," you say. "Don't you recognize it? It's the turban of the wizard's apprentice. We're up here!" you call out.

The boy comes more fully into view, panting up the hill. "Hello!" he calls back, "I was afraid for a while that I had gotten the place where you would reappear mixed up."

He reaches the top of the hill and sits down on a rock, out of breath.

"First, let me introduce myself," says the

boy. "My name is Warkus, and as you know I am—or rather was—the apprentice of the wizard, Zinkor. Just before you left the palace, I overheard him bribing the king's guards that were supposed to protect you as far as the river. Instead, he paid them to kill you. That was the last straw as far as I'm concerned. Zinkor is an evil wizard, and he is allied with Kralux, an even more evil wizard, who lives in the Castle of Doom beyond the mountains."

"Then maybe you know what's going on," Teppin says.

"I don't know all the details," Warkus says, "but I think Zinkor and Kralux are preparing to seize power in the kingdom."

"Does the king know about this?" you ask.

"Not really," says Warkus, "but I think he is beginning to have his suspicions. His kingdom is in turmoil and as you know, one of the royal princesses has been kidnapped."

"*One* of the royal princesses?" Teppin says. "How many are there?"

"An even dozen," Warkus replies.

"Is she the king's favorite?" Thea asks.

"Nor really," says Warkus. "in fact, she is the king's *least* favorite."

"Then I suggest that we give up this foolish quest and find our way to another country," says Teppin.

"No! We can't do that!" Warkus exclaims.

"I'm not sure why, but I think that the fate of this kingdom depends on rescuing the princess."

"Did you say 'we' just now?" you ask. "What did you mean by that?"

Warkus hesitates for a moment, a look of pleading in his eyes. "I'd . . . I'd like to come with you, if . . . if that's all right," he says.

"Now wait a minute!" Teppin exclaims. "I'm not sure what's going on here but—"

"I think it's a good idea," Thea interrupts. "And just because the princess isn't the king's favorite is no reason why we shouldn't try to rescue her."

"I think Thea's right," you say, "and with Warkus along we'll have some backup magic that just might come in very handy."

"Looks like I'm outvoted," Teppin says, laughing. "Welcome aboard," he says to Warkus.

"Let's decide what we're going to do now," you say. "We still have to get across the river."

"I know this area well," says Warkus. "I'm from a small village not far from here. There is a place upriver where it'll be easy to get across. But I think we'd better wait until dark to travel. Zinkor has many soldiers secretly in his employ as well as many spies. And not all of his spies are human."

"Not human?" says Thea.

"He has trained a number of falcons and even some buzzards to fly over the kingdom and report back to him," Warkus says. "With their eagle-like eyes they can spot things—even tiny things—on the ground from miles away."

"You mean the birds can talk?" asks Thea.

"I'm not sure what they do," says Warkus. "It's one of the things Zinkor has refused to teach me."

"There's a grove of trees just down the other side of this hill," you say. "We'll be safe there until dark and also I could use something to eat."

When you are down among the trees, you pull off one of the saddle packs and open it to see what's inside. Not much. Just flat loaves of hard bread, some cheese, and a jug of water. Teppin cuts up the bread and cheese with his knife and passes the pieces around. It tastes pretty good—but maybe that's just because you're very hungry.

As it gets dark, a large, reddish moon rises on the horizon.

"We'll travel as far as we can tonight," you say, "and then we'll sleep during the day tomorrow."

You all start down the hill with Warkus riding on the back of Thea's horse. Soon you reach the river, then head upstream to the spot that Warkus knows about. The horses cross easily in the shallow water.

"We're lucky that the Swirry isn't in flood," says Warkus. "Then the water is much higher and the current is so swift that we would be swept away downstream."

Teppin is the first across. "Over here!" he shouts. "I've found a trail—and it goes east."

The moon is higher now, and brighter. It casts long shadows through the woods.

"We should keep to the shadows as much as possible," says Warkus. "Zinkor's falcons can almost see in the dark."

The horses go at a steady gait, following

the trail through the woods, sometimes around the edges of farms, and rarely out in the open for long periods. You go on this way hour after hour, and by the first faint light of early dawn you are all dozing in the saddle.

"This looks like a good place to rest," you say.

"Rest," Thea says sleepily. "I feel like I could sleep for days."

You all climb down and lead the horses off the trail to a spot surrounded by dense thicket. You lie down on the soft moss on the ground. You are so tired that you doze off immediately.

Suddenly, you find yourself in a dream maze. You realize even in your sleep that you are not *just* dreaming. There is sorcery involved. You try to wake up again—but you can't. You know that you have to get through the maze or you might not wake up at all—ever.

Go to next page.

Find your way through the dream maze. Be careful or your sleep may be a very long one.

Go to page 44
Go to page 110
Start

You wake up lying on the ground. It is late afternoon. Thea is shaking you. "I just had the strangest dream," she says. "I was trapped in this maze and—"

"I know," you say, "I had the same dream. Are Teppin and Warkus all right?"

"*I'm* all right," says Teppin stepping out from behind a tree, "but I can't find any sign of the little wizard."

"I hope Warkus is all right," says Thea.

"I'm sure he is," you say. "He probably just went off to look for something."

"Like some guardsmen, you mean," Teppin says sarcastically.

"That's not fair," Thea says. "Don't forget that he helped us escape from the guardsmen across the river."

"We have to wait until dark anyway," you say. "I'm sure Warkus will be back by that time."

You eat more bread and cheese. You find a clear stream nearby where you can wash up. Later, the sky darkens and the stars start coming out one by one—but still Warkus doesn't come back.

"If we continue on this trail, Warkus will catch up with us," you say. "He seems to have his own way of Travelling when he wants to."

You all remount and start down the trail again. A strong wind starts blowing through the trees and clouds begin to blot out the stars. Then as you come out of the woods, you can see the countryside stretching for miles and miles in the moonlight. Fortunately, the racing clouds soon blot out the bright light of the rising moon.

"Those clouds really look spooky," you say. "They look like dark, giant wings outlined in silver."

"Or two huge hands reaching out to grab us," Thea says.

Soon the trail ends at a main road.

"This part of the country looks pretty deserted," you say. "It might be safe to follow the road for awhile. The moon is behind the clouds and I don't see any farmhouse lights."

The three of you head eastward along the road, carefully watching in front and behind for anyone coming. After an hour or so, you suddenly see dark shapes approaching from the front. They don't seem to be travelling very fast. You all hide behind some large rocks off to one side of the road.

You all feel a little foolish when the dark shapes finally turn into a farmer and his horse-drawn wagon clopping along at a slow pace. You all gallop back to the road.

"Hiieee!" the farmer cries, almost falling off of his wagon.

"Don't be afraid," Thea calls. "We're not

robbers and we won't harm you. We just need some information."

"You gave me quite a start, charging out of the darkness that way," the farmer says.

The moon comes out from behind the clouds for a moment and the farmer gasps.

"By my soul! Too young'uns and a man with a patch," he says. "You're the ones all the fuss is about."

"How is that?" asks Teppin.

"There's a big reward on your heads," says the farmer. "Guard patrols have been searching all the roads. But they're not regular guardsmen. They're renegades. Even I can tell the difference. You're lucky you haven't run into any of them. I've passed two groups of them already tonight. I'd get off of the road if I were you."

"Are there any side roads that might be safe?" Teppin asks.

"Believe me, nowhere is safe as far as you're concerned," says the farmer. "My advice is to go into the barrens over yonder. No one will find you in there. It's a regular maze of hills and gullies."

"What's beyond it?" you ask.

"The town of Butterfield is a half-day's journey to the east. But I wouldn't go near it if I were you. A rebel force is forming there to march against the king. And there's more to it than that." The farmer's voice turns to whisper. "There's supernatural forces at work there too. They say that evil wizards are behind the revolt."

"What kind of supernatural forces," Teppin asks.

"I must be off," the farmer says without answering, panic in his voice—as if he had scared himself by mentioning the wizards. "I'd go straight to the barrens," he calls out as his horses break into a gallop and the wagon disappears into the darkness down the road.

"A fine kettle of fish this is," says Teppin. "We're liable to rescue the princess and then there might not be a kingdom for her to come home to."

"You're right," you say, "It may be only a matter of days before they attack the palace itself."

"Warkus might be right though," says Thea. "If they are so close to taking over the kingdom, why would they bother to kidnap the princess? There must be more to this than meets the eye. And why are *we* so important?"

"And if Zinkor and Kralux do take over the kingdom, there'll be nothing but terror and slavery here," you say.

Suddenly, you see more dark shadows down the road, and this time they're moving fast.

"Quick!" says Teppin, "We've got to get into those barrens before they spot us.

You, Thea, and Teppin gallop your horses across a broad field toward the low hills in the distance. Just as you get to the far side the moon comes out again for a moment. You see

directly in front of you one of the deep gullies leading into the barrens. All of you head for it. You get there just in time. A guard patrol has spotted you in the brief moment of moonlight and is charging across the field in your direction.

Find your way through the barrens—but be careful. There may be things lurking there that you haven't bargained for. And remember, the guardsmen may follow you into the barrens.

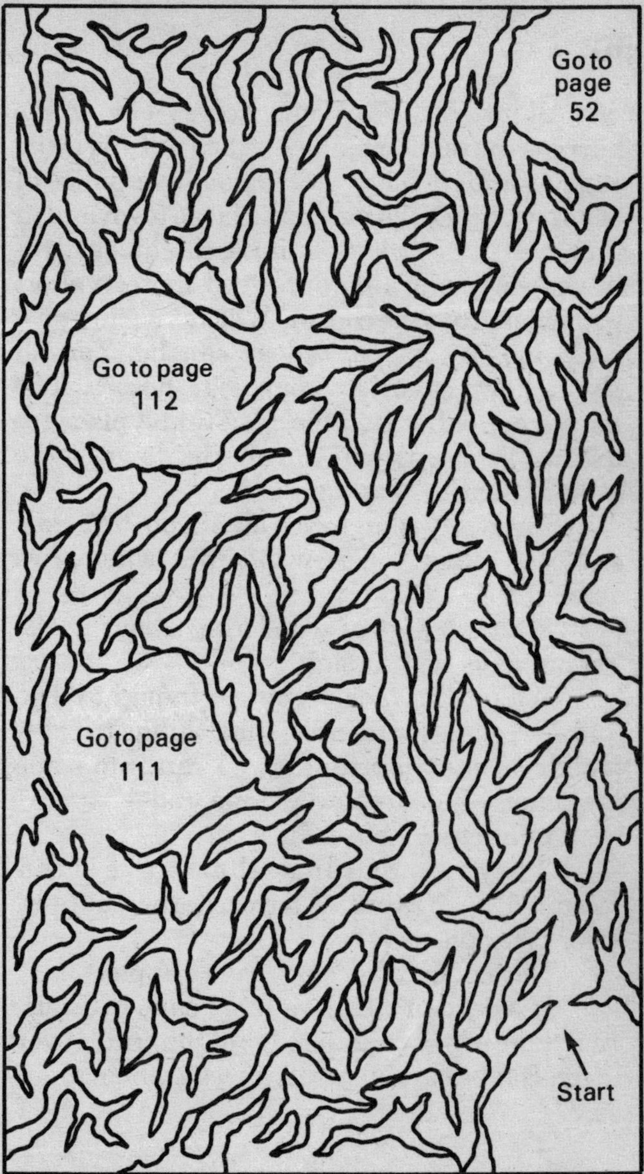
Go to page 52
Go to page 112
Go to page 111
Start

All of you ride your horses out of the barrens maze. You made it! Ahead of you is the edge of a high ridge, looking out over miles of countryside. Down below is a large town and in the far distance a lake, shining like quicksilver in the early morning sun. And there, a short way back from the edge, is Warkus sitting on a rock, looking as relaxed as can be. You all climb down wearily from your horses. The horses are exhausted too. You find a place for them to lie down, then you all sink down on the ground next to Warkus.

"I'm really glad to see all of you," Warkus says, "I guess you're wondering where I've been."

"We *were* sort of wondering about that," Teppin says with a sigh.

"While you were sleeping, I thought I'd go and find some more interesting things to eat—for all of us. Unfortunately, I ran into some granches who overpowered me and—"

"Granches?" says Thea.

"They're creatures that have been recruited by Kralux to terrorize the countryside," Warkus says.

"Never heard of 'em," says Teppin.

"If you don't believe me," says Warkus, "just take a look over the edge of that ridge over there. But be careful, we don't want them to see us."

You go over and carefully peer between some bushes at the edge of the ridge. You see the town down below. It looks deserted. All the windows are shuttered. It reminds you of how Trangor looked as you left the city. However, in the center of the town below is a large square where troops of guardsmen and strange creatures are marching back and forth. At this distance the creatures look tiny, but you can see that they have barbed tails sticking out of the back of their shiny black leather uniforms and pointed ears not quite covered by dark helmets. But more amazing than their appearance, is the way some of them seem to suddenly disappear from one spot and in the same instant reappear in another.

"How do they do that?" you ask Warkus.

"They are operating under the power of Kralux's magic," he answers. "Kralux controls all of their dull minds, and even their physical existence. He does this by projecting his psychic power from his perch in the tower of the Castle of Doom."

"These could be the supernatural creatures that the farmer was so afraid of," you say.

"With all the magic and sorcery that I've learned watching Zinkor, I am powerless against the granches, though I did manage to escape," Warkus says. "They carried me to their headquarters in Butterfield down there and locked me in a room. I heard them talking through the door. They said that you were being hunted in the barrens. I figured that you would probably end up here."

"But how did you get here?" Thea asks.

"There was a small opening at the top of the wall," says Warkus. "I just changed myself into a raven, crawled through the opening, and flew up here."

Changed yourself into a raven?" says Teppin. "Now I've heard everything."

"You think it's easy?" says Warkus. "I'll tell you, I can't do *that* very often. And it was dangerous. With all of Zinkor's falcons flying around, I could have been plucked out of the sky like a pigeon. And speaking of falcons, they must have spotted us by now, which means that this spot won't be safe for very long."

"Warkus is right," you say. "As tired as we are, we've got to keep moving."

"Do you think the horses can take it?" asks Thea.

"We'll just lead them for awhile," Teppin says, "that should help."

"The countryside is swarming with granches, but I think I know a path that will get past them," says Warkus. "We'll go south for a few miles then turn east again and go around the edge of the lake."

You all follow after Warkus. You follow him for hours. You are so tired that you can hardly move, but still you keep going.

"Don't worry," Warkus says. "Once we reach the great forest we'll be safe. The granches won't dare to follow us there."

Now you can see the lake off to the left through the trees. Somehow the sight of it gives you new energy. And suddenly you realize that you're going to need all of the energy that you can get. Loud shouts and grunts are coming toward you along the path you just travelled.

"They've got our scent!" Warkus shouts. "Let's ride to the forest as fast as we can."

You all mount up with Warkus behind Thea again. The horses take you down the trail at a gallop.

"How far is it?" you shout.

"We should get to the edge of the great forest in about an hour if the horses can keep up this pace."

Warkus and Thea take the lead with Warkus telling her where to direct her horse. Some of his directions seem meaningless until you realize that he is following an almost invisible trail. Even Teppin is beginning to look at him with a kind of admiration.

Finally, you head out into a wide expanse of grass. Up ahead the edge of the forest is like

a huge wall rising suddenly out of the earth. You are halfway across the fields when a huge horde of granches pours out of the woods behind you. Suddenly, one of them pops out of nowhere and appears in front of you.

"Don't try to fight them!" Warkus shouts. "Just try to run your horses around and past them. They can't move very fast.

Granches are appearing all over the place. But once they appear, they seem to move in slow motion.

"We're almost there—don't give up now!" Warkus calls back.

So many granches are appearing that you seem to be running some kind of crazy obstacle course.

Then almost before you realize it, you are into the forest. The granches, as Warkus had predicted, don't come in after you. Huge trees rise all around you like a majestic cathedral. Except for the panting of the horses, all is silent. The forest stretches like a giant maze toward the mountains.

Go to next page.

Find your way through the forest maze. Remember that the forest has its own dangers—so be careful.

Start
Go to page 60
Go to page 113
Go to page 114

You and your friends leave the forest behind. Ahead lies a desert landscape, strewn here and there with boulders. In the far distance, the jagged outline of the blue mountains rises into the sky. From one of the peaks, a plume of dark smoke drifts upward.

"That smoke comes from the fiery mountain," Warkus says, "I often heard my family talk of it when I was younger. Kralux's castle is not far beyond it."

You start to ride in that direction. But the ground is covered with round pebbles and the horses' hooves start to slip on them. After going a few yards, you realize that it's no use and dismount. Leading the horses, you all go on for an hour or so. The horses' hooves crunch along on the stones. The desert—with its pebbles and huge boulders—seems to go on forever. Then suddenly, you come to the edge of a deep canyon. It stretches as far as you can see east and west, and it's many leagues across. You look down at the sheer drop of hundreds of feet.

A movement catches your eye behind you. You could swear that you saw one of the boulders move.

"Did you see that?" you ask Teppin.

"I did indeed!" he says.

"Look! There's another!" Thea exclaims.

A wide circle of the boulders starts to move

with a grinding noise—in your direction!

"I'm not sure what's happening," you say, "but I think we should get out of here as fast as we can."

"But where can we go?" asks Thea. "Whatever they are, they have us surrounded!"

"Let's run between them," you say.

"Wait!" shouts Teppin. "That may be just what they're trying to get us to do."

"What they want to do," says Thea, "is to push us off this cliff."

"You all stay here and I'll take a quick look," says Warkus, and before you can stop him he runs out between two of the moving boulders. Suddenly a huge figure—twice the size of a man and with an ugly, reptilian face—steps out and makes a grab for him. Warkus springs away just in time and comes running back.

"It's a knar!" he says, out of breath. "I've never seen a real one before, but I've heard plenty of stories. There's one behind each of those boulders pushing them."

Suddenly, a fist-sized rock whizzes by your head. You see the head of the knar that threw it duck back behind the boulder. Then another knar jumps out, hurls a rock, and jumps back.

"They're huge!" Thea exclaims. "Why aren't they just rushing us themselves?"

"They may be afraid that we have

crossbows or some weapons that they don't know about," Warkus says.

"Speaking of weapons," you say, as you pull your slingshot from your belt, "I'm going to give them a taste of their own medicine."

Just as a knar jumps out to throw, you catch him squarely between the eyes with a stone. The knar grunts and staggers back for a moment, more from surprise than anything else. Then you hit him in the side of the head with another stone. He swats at it the way you would swat at a fly. Your next stone hits him in the chest just as he is about to let fly with a rock. The rock goes sailing off to the side.

"At least I'm spoiling his aim," you say.

Unfortunately, the next rock from a knar hits your horse in the flank—then another lands on a foreleg. The horse rears backwards, and before you can grab the bridle, the horse goes careening off the edge of the cliff, tumbling end over end until it finally hits the bottom of the canyon far below.

The other two horses are hit also. They panic and try to gallop away between the boulders, where they are grabbed and dragged out of sight by the knars.

"There go our poor horses!" Thea cries.

"Not to mention all our supplies," Teppin adds.

"This is no time to worry about horses or

supplies," you say, "we've got to get off of this cliff or we'll follow that horse over the edge."

Then you notice that Warkus is on his stomach leaning out over the edge of the cliff. "Look," he says, "there's another ledge below this one. If we can swing down. . . ."

One of the knars is up on the top of one of the boulders about to throw down a big stone. In a flash, Thea's whip is wrapped around his ankles. The knar loses his balance and goes crashing back behind the boulder. There is silence for a few moments, then what sounds like confused, murmuring sounds from that direction.

"Quick!" says Teppin. "I think Thea's whip has them puzzled for the moment. I'll swing each of you down to the lower level, then follow—while we have the chance."

Teppin's powerful arms swing each of you underneath. Then he gets set to swing down himself. But, as he does, a rock from a recovered knar crashes into his shoulder. Teppin grunts in pain and slips down using the other arm. You and Thea manage to grab him just in time to prevent him from falling into the canyon.

Fortunately, the ledge goes deep underneath the top of the cliff. You help Teppin lie down, and look at this shoulder. There is a deep, nasty gash. Warkus tears off part of his

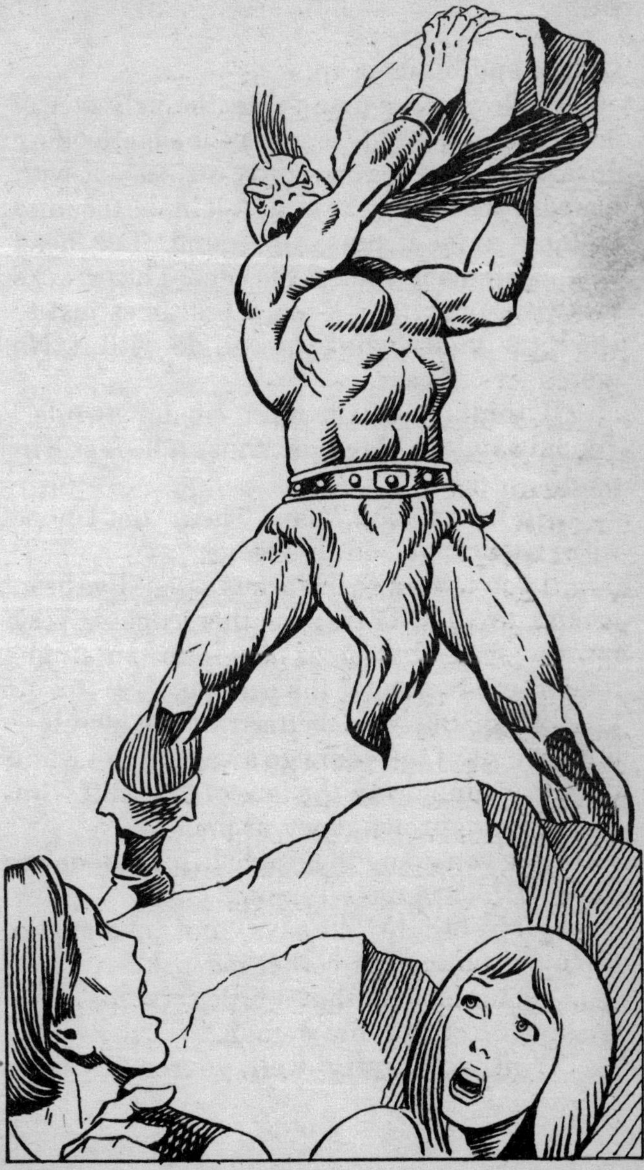

turban and binds it up.

While you are doing this, the ugly face of one of the knars appears over the edge, looking down at you. Thea instantly strikes out with her whip, catching the knar full in the face and making a loud, cracking sound. The head disappears back behind the edge. Thea cracks her whip in the air a few more times just to show the knars what she can do with it. No more faces appear.

"I think that will hold 'em for awhile," Teppin says, smiling now, though he is still in pain.

"So far so good," says Thea, "but I hope we're not trapped on this ledge."

"I don't think so," Warkus says. "I've been looking around. There's another ledge—a very narrow one—that goes down at an angle toward the bottom of the canyon."

"Good! But we'd better rest for awhile—and also see if the knars go away. I don't want to be crawling down the face of that cliff with rocks being thrown down at me."

"Are you going to be able to make it down the cliff?" Thea asks Teppin.

"I'll be alright," he says, "I'm not going to let this little scratch bother me."

"I'd hardly call that a little scratch," says Warkus. "You're a brave man."

"You did pretty well yourself," says

Teppin, "especially when we were escaping from the granches."

"Thanks," Warkus says.

All is quiet for awhile. You all try to rest the best you can. You realize that it isn't going to be easy going down the cliff.

Later, you all get yourselves together and start down one by one. Teppin, despite his wound, insists on going first, followed by Warkus and Thea. You follow.

You are not sure how long it takes to get to the bottom of the canyon, but it seems like hours. As you get near the bottom, the roar of the rapids below gets louder and louder. Finally, you are all down. A wide, sandy path runs beside the fast-flowing river.

"We'll head east down the river and see where it goes," you say.

"I sure hope these canyon walls start to get lower rather than higher," says Thea.

Suddenly, there is a loud crash almost like an explosion nearby. Something makes you look up to the top of the cliff. There you can see the now tiny figures of the knars preparing to push another boulder off of the top. You realize what the crash was—a boulder falling from above.

"Hurry!" shouts Teppin, "If we move fast, they won't be able to zero in on us with those rocks."

No more rocks fall, but as you all run along the side of the river, the figures above keep up with you. Then up ahead, you see a large opening into the base of the cliff.

"I wonder what that is," you say.

"It could be a cave, or maybe an entrance to a cavern," says Teppin.

"I have a hunch that it may be a way to get out of the canyon," Warkus says.

Soon you are at the entrance to whatever it is. You look inside. You find yourselves in a large, round, and naturally domed room. At the far side of it is the start of a tunnel.

Warkus sits crosslegged and with his eyes closed in the center of the room. You watch him in silence. After a few minutes, Warkus opens his eyes and smiles.

"I see in my mind a maze of underground tunnels," he says. "At their end is a way out near the foot of the mountains. There are dangers here also, but I think it's worth a try."

You all agree to go through the maze. You find some sticks, their ends coated with pitch, that are obviously meant to be torches. Teppin, fortunately, has his flints with him and he easily starts the torches burning. Each of you takes one and you start into the tunnels.

Go to next page.

Find your way through the tunnel maze. But don't forget about the dangers that Warkus saw in his vision.

Go to page 72
Go to page 115
Start →

You come out of the tunnel and into the bright daylight. The mountains are so close that they tower above you. Only a gently rolling, grassy moor a few miles across separates you from their base. High above, a broad plume of smoke from the fiery mountain curls into the sky. Oddly enough, a stone-paved path leads straight as an arrow from the tunnel exit toward the mountains.

'This must be a well-travelled route to have such a good path," says Teppin.

"It seems a little too good to be true," says Warkus. "I sense no danger, but I think we should be very careful."

"It shouldn't take long to get to the mountains," says Thea. "I almost feel that I could reach out and touch them."

You all start off, feeling glad to be out in the open with the blue sky overhead—particularly after being cooped up in those underground tunnels. You go up and down over the low, rolling hills for almost an hour.

"Those mountains are further away than I thought," says Thea.

"I know," says Teppin, "but we're definitely getting closer."

Then suddenly, at the top of one of the hills, you find yourself looking down into a beautiful valley. Here and there are small, azure blue lakes set in a thick carpet of bright green grass and surrounded by groves of flowering dogwood trees.

In the center of the valley, close to the road, is a charming little cottage, looking a bit like an oversized doll house. Around it are carefully tended flower gardens.

"I've never seen anything so perfect!" Thea exclaims.

"That's what I'm worried about," says Warkus. "It's a little too perfect."

"You mean it's an illusion?" you say.

"No, it seems real enough," says Warkus, "It's just that—"

Warkus stops in mid-sentence as an old woman appears, standing by the door of the house.

"We have to be careful," Warkus whispers. "That woman is a witch, though whether a good one or a bad one I can't tell from here."

All of you start down the hill, still impressed by the beauty of the valley, but you are all worried about the witch.

"What should we do?" Teppin whispers to Warkus. "You know more about these things than we do."

"I guess the only thing we can do, is play along," says Warkus. "Try to humor her. Maybe she'll let us go on our way without any trouble."

You are close enough now to see the witch

clearly. She looks pleasant enough with her hair tied in a flower-printed cloth and wearing a black and white checkered apron.

"Ah! Weary travellers I see," she calls out as you approach the cottage. "Come into my house and take some refreshments before you go any further."

"Should we accept her offer?" you whisper to Warkus.

"I'm not sure myself," Warkus whispers back. "But if we turn her down, we might have an angry witch on our hands—and one thing I *do* know is that it's not good to get them mad."

"She looks so sweet," Thea whispers. "Are you sure that she's a witch?

"Well, experience is the best teacher someone told me once. After you," Warkus says, making a flourish with his hand toward the door of the cottage.

You all go in. It is even smaller on the inside than it looked on the outside. The woman leads you in to a tiny kitchen where you all squeeze around a small, circular table. Oddly enough, the curtains on the windows are drawn. But there is still plenty of light coming through them. A tall candle is lit at the center of the table.

"Let me get you some cakes and juice," the woman says. She disappears through the door and seconds later reappears with a tray full of

pastries.

"They're all right to eat," Warkus whispers, "I would sense it if they were poisoned."

You all eat the cakes. They are delicious, and you feel strangely refreshed after eating them.

Then suddenly, the door to the kitchen slams shut. There is a loud bang at each of the windows and they go dark. The only light now is from the candle on the table. A loud, demonic laugh comes from the other side of the door.

"Now that you've eaten my cakes," the witch screeches, "it's time for you to pay the price." Then there is more of her awful laughter; it seems to fill the room all around you.

Teppin rushes over and pulls open the kitchen door. The rest of the house has vanished and a long corridor has taken its place. At the same time, you yank back the curtains covering the windows. The outside is blocked with a wall of solid stone.

"What's going on!" Thea exclaims.

"The house has turned into a witch's maze," says Warkus. "But don't worry, we'll find our way out of it."

"Is it dangerous?" you ask.

"Well, there are liable to be, uh, let's say . . . unexpected things," says Warkus.

"Unexpected things!" says Teppin, laughing. "That's a good way of putting it. But, we might as well get started."

You take the candle from the table and start down the corridor. At the far end, it divides, one section going left and the other going right. You are into the maze.

Go to next page.

Find your way through the witch's maze. But remember what Warkus said about "unexpected things."

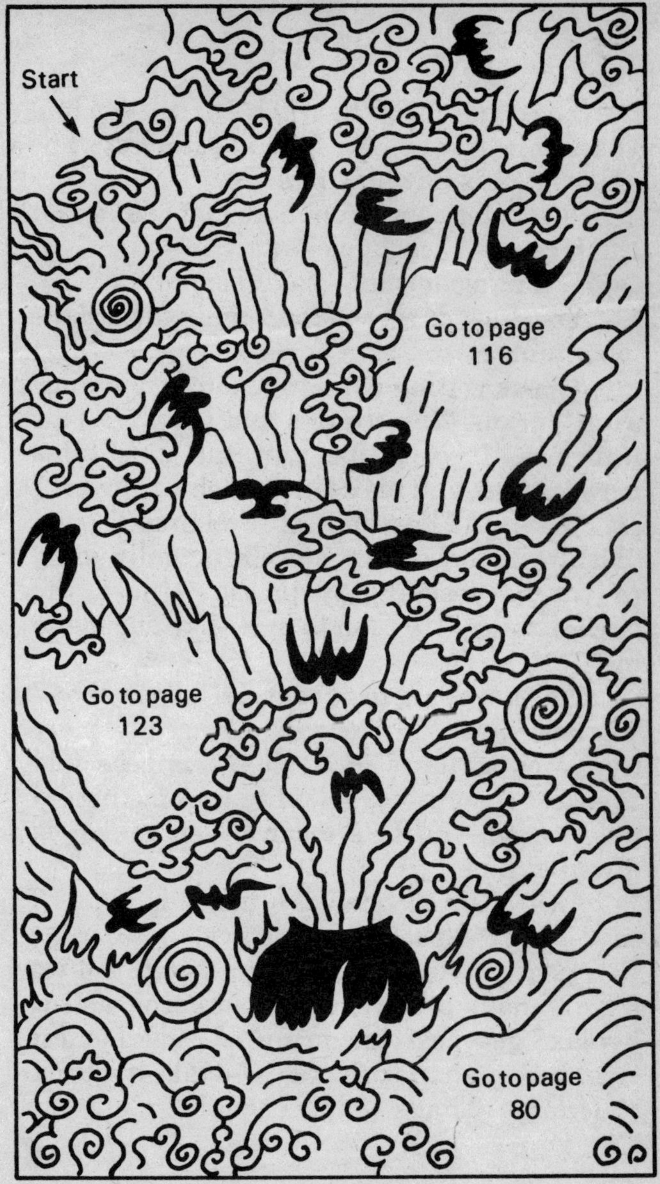

Start
Go to page 116
Go to page 123
Go to page 80

You come out of the witch's maze. You find yourself in front of the little house again. The old woman is nowhere in sight.

"Let's get away from here fast before that witch comes back," you say.

"I'll agree to that," says Teppin.

You start down the road again toward the mountains.

"We're getting close to Kralux's domain," says Warkus. "It's strange that I don't feel his influence. It could be that the mountains between here and his castle somehow block it."

"Kralux! The princess!" exclaims Teppin. "I'd almost forgotten that we're actually going to try to rescue a princess. Under the circumstances, it sounds more like suicide to me."

"It's not going to be easy, I'll tell you that," Warkus says. "My powers are really puny compared to those of Kralux. I've been told that just his gaze can set fire to something a mile away. And he's mean. Even Zinkor is afraid of him."

"We've faced obstacles like this before," says Thea. "We'll do it somehow."

"Sure," says Teppin with a laugh. All we have to do is get over the mouintains, defeat Kralux, get past his army of superhuman creatures, grab the princess, and take her back to Trangor. That's simple enough."

The mountains loom larger and larger ahead. You can already see what looks like a trail going up the side of the fiery mountain.

"That way looks as good as any," says Teppin.

"It seems to branch off high up there," says Thea.

"We'll find our way," says Warkus, "as long as we're careful.

Go to next page.

Find your way through the mountain maze.

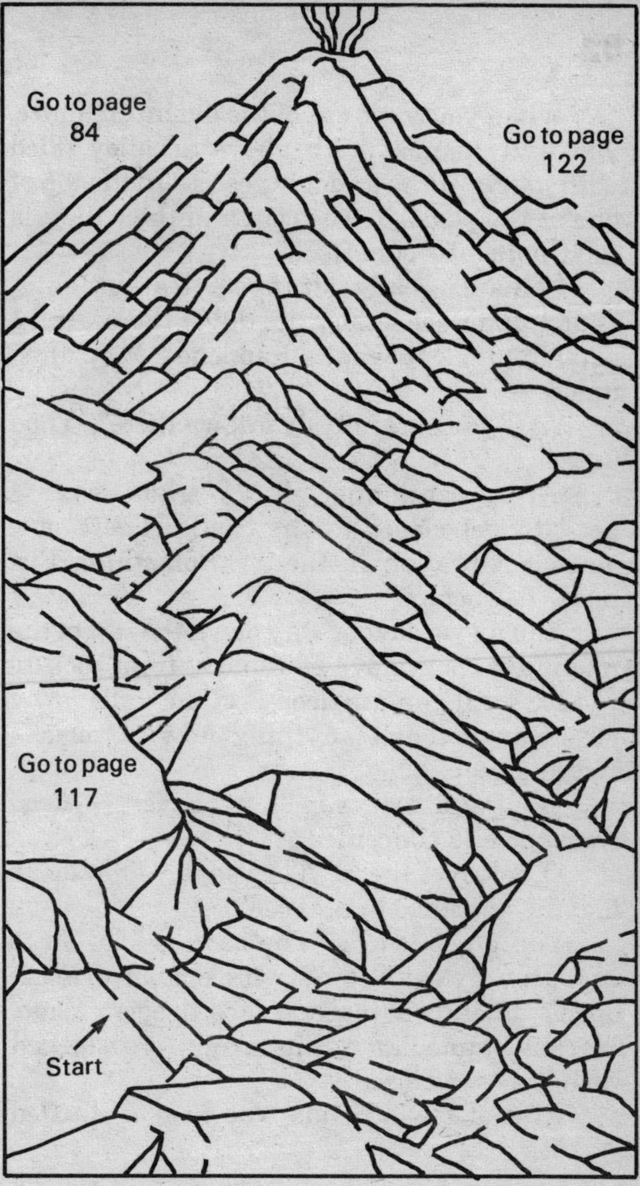
Go to page
84
Go to page
122
Go to page
117
Start

When you come out of the mountain maze, you find yourself high above a valley filled with jagged rocks and low peaks. On the top of one of the peaks, in the center of the valley, is the Castle of Doom itself.

"This is really strange," Warkus says, "but I don't sense any life down there. And I can't figure out what's happened to Kralux, unless—"

"Are you sure nobody's down there?" Thea asks.

"Well, not completely," Warkus says. "I need to get closer to the castle. There *is* a strange vibration in the air. Something I've never felt before."

You all work your way down the rest of the mountain. You move cautiously from rock to to rock until you are deep into the valley.

"Can you tell anything now?" you ask Warkus.

"I'm still not sure," he says, "I need someplace to concentrate."

"Look over there!" Thea says. "That looks like the entrance to a cave."

You go over to it. The cave is just large enough to crawl into near the entrance, but it opens up into a larger space deeper inside. Warkus immediately sits down crosslegged with his eyes closed.

After a few seconds, you hear a startled

gasp from Warkus. Even in the dim light inside the cave you can see that his face has turned pale.

"This . . . this is awful!" he exclaims.

"What is?" Thea asks.

"I . . . I don't even know if I can describe it," Warkus says, "but we've got to get into the castle as fast as we can. We have to stop Kralux before it's too late."

"What about the guards?" Teppin asks.

"That's one thing we don't have to worry about," Warkus says, "Kralux has put them all into a temporary state of deep sleep, until he has his "new form," which will be very soon. We are lucky for the moment. This is the one time—every three hundred years—when Kralux is vulnerable."

I don't understand what you mean by new form," Teppin says.

"No time to explain," Warkus says. "If we don't get to the castle right away, the princess as she exists now will be gone, Kralux will be safe for another three hundred years, and the kingdom will be doomed."

"All right, let's go!" says Teppin, leading the way out of the cave and across the stretch of jagged rocks to the castle.

"How do you figure we're going to get in?" you ask Teppin as you run along beside him.

"Don't worry," he says. "Every castle has

its weak point and I'll find it. Remember that I know castles the way Warkus knows magic."

When you get to the castle wall, you follow Teppin running around its base. He stops suddenly and points up. "There it is," he says. "The way in."

"I don't see—" starts Thea as she catches up with you.

"There's a small hole up there on the wall," Teppin says, "it's just big enough for us to crawl through."

Teppin climbs up first on your shoulders to reach the hole and squeezes in. Warkus and Thea follow. Then Thea lowers the length of her whip and you use it to climp up.

You find yourselves in a dimly lit corridor inside the castle.

"Now we have to find Kralux—and the princess," Teppin says. "They're probably in the throne room."

Find your way through the castle maze to the throne room. But hurry, Kralux's powers are about to return.

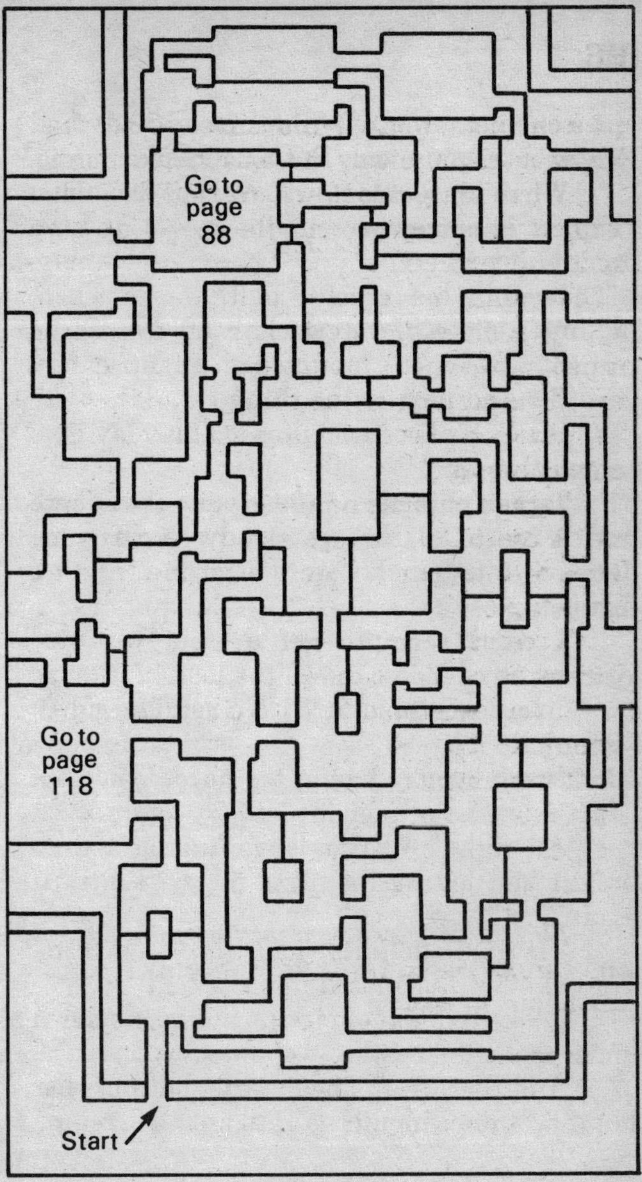
Go to page 88
Go to page 118
Start

You get through the maze and find Kralux's throne room. But no Kralux.

"We're in trouble now!" Warkus exclaims. "Kralux is somewhere in the castle and we don't know where."

"Is this his crystal ball?" asks Thea, pulling a piece of velvet cloth off of a large transparent sphere, mounted on an intricately carved stand next to the throne.

"It is!" Warkus exclaims. "This may give us our answer."

Warkus puts his hands around the sphere and it starts to become cloudy—as if some dense, white smoke were swirling around inside.

"I can't seem to get a clear picture," Warkus says. You can see the look of intense concentration on his face. "No use," he sighs, "I can't do it."

"Maybe you're trying too hard," you say. "Just relax for a moment and try again."

"All right," Warkus says, taking a deep breath and letting his arms relax. "I'll try it again."

This time a definite picture begins to form. You all stare fascinated into the ball.

"Looks like a room in the dungeons down underneath the castle," Teppin says.

"And there's—" Thea starts, but puts her hand up to her mouth as if to stop a scream.

"Horrible!" Teppin exclaims.

"We've got to get there and—" you say.

Suddenly, a side door to the throne room flies open and the tall form of Zinkor steps out.

"So you want to go down to the dungeons, do you," he snarls. "I'll see to it that you all go down there—permanently. And *you*, Warkus, you little traitor—after I taught you nearly everything I know."

Zinkor takes a short crystalline rod from his sleeve and aims it at Warkus. Warkus is thrown back against the wall as if tossed there by a giant hand. He is dazed, clutching his throat and gasping for breath.

Zinkor doesn't see Thea slipping her whip from her belt. In a flash, Thea strikes out with it, yanking the rod out of Zinkor's hand. With a chiming sound, the rod bounces a few times on the stone floor and rolls toward Teppin. Teppin scoops it up and, as Zinkor rushes at him, tosses it to Warkus, who is now free.

"Give me that you little—" shouts Zinkor, as he turns to run after Warkus.

It is at this moment that you hit Zinkor smack in the side of the head with one of your best slingshot stones. Teppin catches him as he falls and lays him out neatly on the floor.

"He'll be out cold for awhile," you say. "Now lets find that dungeon room before it's too late."

"Right," says Warkus, "that door that Zinkor came through must lead down to the dungeons."

Go to next page.

Find your way through the dungeon maze to where Kralux is holding the princess captive. But be careful. There still may be dangers down there you don't know about.

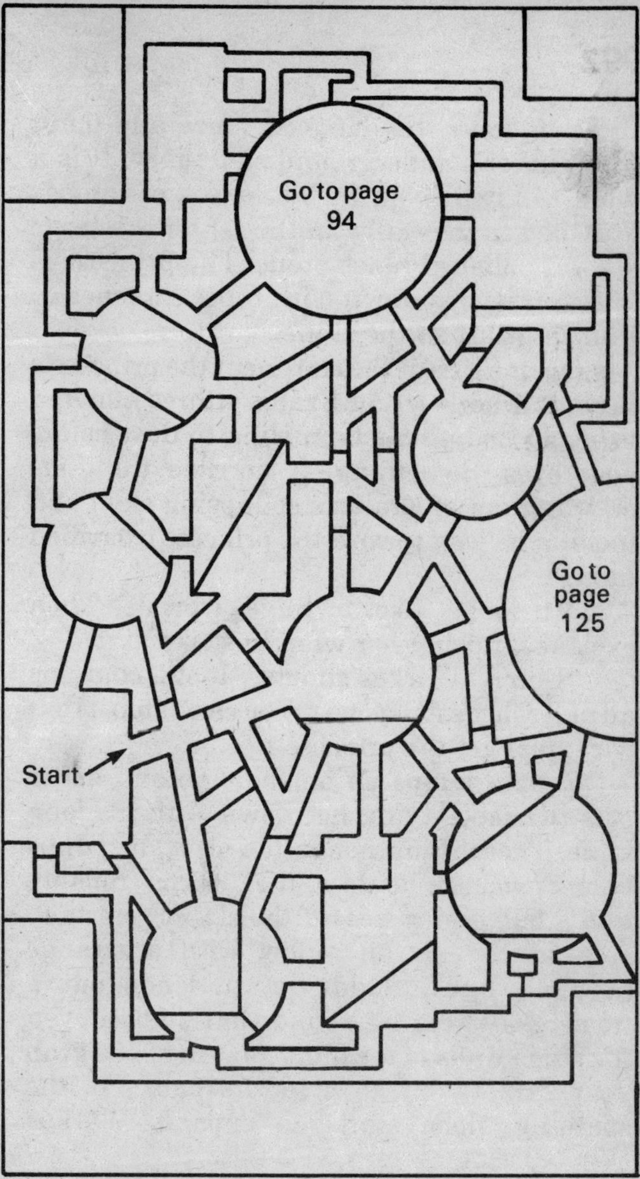
Go to page 94
Go to page 125
Start

You solve the dungeon maze and burst into Zinkor's underground sanctuary. It is a wide, vaulted room lit by dozens of torches attached to the walls. In the center is a large slab of polished black stone. The princess is lying on it, tied down with ropes attached to iron rings set in the stone.

On one side of the slab, near the princess's head, is what's left of Kralux's three hundred year old body, now crumbling to dust before your eyes. Something—a horrible thing—is crawling out of Kralux's collapsing skull and inching its way toward the princess's terrified face.

"It looks like a huge worm!" Thea exclaims, raising her whip to strike at it.

"Don't!" Warkus shouts. "It still contains all of Kralux's evil power. You can't stop it that way. Just get the princess free."

Teppin jumps up on the slab and deftly cuts the ropes tying her down with his long knife. Then lifting her in his arms, he jumps back down. As he does, the "worm" rolls up into a ball and raises off the slab. It starts to spin in the air and glow with a strange purplish light. Suddenly, it sends out a tremendous roaring sound that shakes even the stone walls of the dungeon. All of you grab your ears to try to stop the pain. As the spinning globe starts to expand, Warkus motions with his hand toward the door of the chamber. His face has an expression of agony as he runs toward it. You're not feeling too good yourself. Your brain feels like it's about to explode.

Somehow, you all get out and slam the heavy iron doors to the chamber shut. Seconds later, a tremendous force crashes into the other side of the doors, almost tearing them from their hinges. The metal starts to glow a dull red from the intense heat inside. The walls around you are shaking.

With Teppin still carrying the princess, you all dash back down the dungeon corridors. Fortunately, it doesn't take you long to find your way back to the main level of the castle and then to the small opening where you first crawled in. Thc whole castle is now shaking violently. One of its towers collapses with a roar.

"Let's get back to that cave over there!" Warkus shouts, "we have only seconds before the castle blows up."

You dive into the cave just as a tremendous explosion tears the castle to pieces. The shock of the explosion knocks the breath out of you and all of you lie there stunned on the floor of the cave. Some of the heavy stones blown from the castle crash down around the entrance of the cave, sealing you inside.

Then silence and darkness.

"Whew! That was close," says Teppin.

"We still have a few problems," you say. "Like being buried alive and with no light."

"I think I may have the answer to the light problem," says Warkus, pulling Zinkor's crystal rod from under his cloak. Immediately the whole inside of the cave is lit up with light from the rod. You notice a small opening at the back of the cave.

"I sense that through that opening lies a maze of underground passageways that will lead us back to safety," says Warkus. "It won't take us long."

"First," says Thea, "I'd like to know one thing. What would've happened if we hadn't rescued the princess here in time?"

"Oh, that's simple," says Warkus. "That 'worm' that you saw was a form of Kralux's brain. It would have bored its way into the princess's lovely head and promptly eaten her brain, replacing it. Then the kingdom would have an evil, all-powerful queen for the next three hundred years."

The princess puts her face in her hands and starts to sob.

"Now, look here," says Teppin. "We saved you, didn't we?"

"Leave her alone," says Thea. "How would you like it if your brain was almost eaten by a giant worm."

"Good point," Teppin says. "Let's get through this underground maze so that we can all get back to Trangor.

Find your way through the underground maze.

Go to page
100
Go to page
126
Start

At the end of the underground maze, you find yourselves in a cavern. An underground river is flowing through it.

"Look, there's a boat tied up over there," Teppin says. "Let's take a chance and see where this stream goes."

You all climb in the boat and cast off. The princess is feeling better now, even smiling now and then, particularly when Warkus happens to look in her direction.

"I'll be so glad to get home," she says. "It was so nice of daddy to send you to rescue me. I used to wonder if he really cared about me."

After floating on the river current for awhile, you see a shaft of daylight up ahead and soon the boat emerges into the sunlight.

"I think I recognize where we are," says Warkus. "This is a stream that flows way around the mountains to the south. It eventually flows into the Swirry."

"What a lovely way to travel," says the princess, clearly relieved.

"Further downstream, you come to a small village. There you learn that all the granches and other semi-human monsters that had been terrorizing the countryside have suddenly and miraculously vanished. The villagers recognize the princess and load up your boat with supplies.

The rest of the trip home—a little over a

week—is more of a picnic than anything else. When you finally get back to Trangor, you find that peace and order have been restored. The people are in the streets, celebrating.

Sometime later, Warkus is appointed the new royal sorcerer. The king seems happy to have his daughter back, even if she is his least favorite.

"Congratulations on the rescue," says the king. "By the way, did you get your donkey cart and spices back? No? I'll have it seen to right away." The king turns to one of his advisors with a stern look. "Now I must be off to a big party being given in my honor," says the king as he vanishes out the door of the throne room.

"Some thanks we got for saving his kingdom," says Teppin.

"Don't worry," says the princess, "when *I'm* queen someday.... Anyway, you'll always be welcome in Trangor."

THE END

"This maze is harder than I thought it would be," you say.

"I think we've been going around in circles," Thea says, "I left a mark on one of these pillars awhile back and—"

"Hold it a second," you say. "What was that sound just then?"

You both listen. You hear a low grunt and what sounds like hooves pawing the dirt floor.

"What could it be?" asks Thea.

"I have a hunch," you say, "but I hope I'm wrong. Remember that story we heard on one of the islands about a monster—half-human and half-bull. There was something about a labyrinth."

"Labyrinth is another name for a maze, isn't it?" Thea says, her voice suddenly afraid.

Then, looking behind you, Thea lets out a scream that echoes through the passageways. You turn and see a huge shape, the upper half that of a bull and the lower half that of a man—a giant man. The creature is charging at you. You try to jump to one side, but the corridor is too narrow. The beast spears you through the heart with one of its long, sharp horns, then tosses you like a rag doll back over its shoulder.

THE END

If you don't like this ending, go back to page 20 and try again.

"This doesn't look like the market square to me!" exclaims Thea.

"We must have missed it," you say, "We'll have to go back."

But before you can turn around a sharp command comes from behind you. "Stand where you are!" someone orders.

At the same time, several soldiers with crossbows step out of the darkness around you.

"Looks like we've caught another couple of spies," says the voice. "Tie them up."

You and Thea get ready to spring into action—but you realize that it's no use. There are too many of them, and they have their crossbows aimed at your hearts. You have no choice but to allow yourselves to be tied up and led away.

The soldiers take you to the castle and then down into the dark dungeons below. You will be there for a long, long time.

THE END

If you don't like this ending, go back to page 10 and try again.

You thread your way through the maze for what seems like hours. Finally, you see a bright light at the end of one of the passageways. You and Thea head in that direction. Suddenly, Thea grabs you and pulls you off to the side.

"What...? you say.

"That's Zinkor down there!" Thea whispers. "I have a feeling that we shouldn't let him see us."

"You're right," you say, peering cautiously around a pillar.

Zinkor has some kind of rod in his hand and is tracing an invisible diagram in the air. Well, not quite invisible. An image of white light is forming in the air in front of him. Then the image starts to spin like a small whirlwind, showering sparks around it and making a loud, crackling sound. It starts to drift through the air in your direction.

You and Thea quickly retreat, but as you turn a corner in the maze, another one of the brightly glowing whirlwinds blocks your path. You try another direction, but there is another whirlwind waiting for you. This one is close enough that you can feel its intense heat.

Go to next page.

Then suddenly, all of the whirling columns of flame rush at you—trapping you in the middle. There is a terrible explosion as you are disintegrated.

THE END

If you don't like this ending, go back to page 20 and try again.

You wend your way through the illusion maze. It's not easy. The luminous walls seem to be flowing past you. But they are solid enough, you try but you can't push your way through them.

"Up ahead there!" shouts Thea. "Is that the end of the maze or just another part of it?"

"I'm not sure," you say. "Let's take a look—but carefully."

You and Thea go through. It's more like an opening in a moving curtain than a door. You find yourselves in a beautiful garden, with row upon row of brightly colored flowers stretching to the horizon. A winding path leads from where you are standing into the far distance.

"It's wonderful!" Thea exclaims.

"It's also an illusion," Teppin reminds her. "We'd better get back into the regular part of the maze."

But it's too late. The maze has vanished. The flowerbeds now stretch in multicolored profusion in all directions.

"Way over there, on the path!" Thea exclaims. "It's a figure. I can't make out who it is, but it's beckoning to us to follow it."

You can't see it clearly either. The figure is surrounded and partially hidden by a bright halo of light.

"It could be Warkus," Thea says hopefully.

"Or Zinkor leading us into a trap," you say. "In any event, we don't have much choice except to go and see who it is."

You all start out, but as you try to get close to the figure, it seems to get father and farther away. You go on like this for hours and hours. After a long while you realize that the chase is hopeless. But you can't seem to stop. In fact, you will go on and on chasing this illusion for years and years.

THE END

If you don't like this ending, go back to page 34 and try again.

You seem to be moving through the dream maze in slow motion. Images appear for a moment and then vanish, images of strange castles and vast armies of horsemen. The walls of the maze curl into arabesque-like shapes and in places seem almost transparent. From time to time you are sure that you see Zinkor's evil face leering at your from the other side.

Something deep in your mind tells you that you have to wake up or you will be trapped in the dream forever. You pinch yourself as hard as you can—but you can't feel anything! Then your body shakes as if some strong force were being applied to your shoulders.

"Wake up! Wake up!" someone is shouting from far away. You recognize the voice. It's Teppin's. Then you hear Thea shouting the same thing.

You *try* to wake up, but you can't. You are trapped in the dream forever!

THE END

If you don't like this ending, go back to page 42 and try again.

Finding your way through the barrens turns out to be hard going. The sides of the hills are too steep for your horses to climb up and the passageways between them are sometimes just wide enough to squeeze through. You keep having to double back. From time to time you hear the shouts of the guardsmen in the distance as they search for you. Sometimes they are close, sometimes far away.

Later, you come out onto a broad space somewhere in the center of the barrens. At the same moment the moon comes out from behind the clouds and bathes you in bright light. A shout goes up from the other side of the clearing as a detail of guardsmen spots you and starts their charge. You, Teppin, and Thea all turn your horses around for a dash back into the ravine.

But you don't have time. The guardsmen are already on top of you. The one in the lead decapitates you with a deft slash of his sword. Your head goes flying up into the air and then down again—bouncing once on the ground and rolling into the dark shadows as the moon goes back into the clouds.

THE END

If you don't like this ending, go back to page 50 and try again.

The barrens prove treacherous in more ways than one. The "trails" between the hills get narrower and narrower until the horses can't get through. Then they can't turn around either—they can only back up. Other places where the trail is wide enough to get through easily, the sandy ground gets so soft that the horses' hooves start to sink in.

Then you come to a wide, round, open area shaped like a large bowl. The smooth, sandy ground sinks down in the middle.

"I don't like the looks of this place," Teppin says. "We'd better go back and look for another way through."

You are about to do just that, when you hear the angry shouts of guardsmen not far behind you.

"Looks like we'll have to go this way whether we like it or not," you say.

You all start across. Halfway to the other side, you realize your mistake—the horses start quickly sinking into quicksand. They struggle against it, but this only makes them sink faster. The terrified screams of the horses are cut short as their heads sink beneath the sand.

Not long afterwards your head follows.

THE END

If you don't like this ending, go back to page 50 and try gain.

The forest turns out to be dark and gloomy. The high branches of the trees intertwine high overhead and cut off most of the light. Here and there a narrow shaft of light streams down from a slight break in the forest canopy.

"It sure is spooky in here," Thea says.

"I sense danger around us," Warkus says. "Still, I'm not exactly sure what it's from. I do know that creatures of some sort have been following us high up in the trees."

As you go on, the look on Warkus's face is more and more worried. Suddenly, he cries out, "We must go back as fast as we can!"

You all start to turn your horses, but at the same moment a large number of ropes drop from above and curl themselves around you. In the next moment, you are yanked from your horse and pulled up into the air. You look and see large, hideous creatures with huge, gaping mouths, pulling you up. They are hauling all of you in like minnows out of a pond. You arrived just in time for dinner—theirs.

THE END

If you don't like this ending, go back to page 58 and try again.

You all ride through the dark, dank forest. The trunks of the trees rise up out of the ground like enormous pillars soaring hundreds of feet into the air. There is little undergrowth, few bushes or small trees, but as you get deeper into the forest, long, thick vines begin to hang down from above. In some places they curl around the trunks of the trees like a necklace of serpents. You could swear that some of the vines swayed toward you as you passed.

Suddenly, some vines break loose over your heads and come crashing down around you like a huge net. But *this* net is alive. Thick tendrils wrap around and immediately start to crush you. Teppin slashes away with his long knife, cutting some of them loose. But there are too many for him, and soon even his strong arm is immobilized by the many loops of living vine.

There is no escape. Soon the vines have you completely encased in their coils and are crushing your lifeless body.

THE END

If you don't like this ending, go back to page 58 and try again.

The torchlight flickers eerily down the long, curving stretches of the tunnel. The walls are smooth—almost polished. Every once in a while, you come to a dead end, but you easily retrace your steps and keep going forward. The steady rhythm of your footsteps echos through the underground chambers.

Suddenly, a roar booms through the tunnel up ahead. You are about to run back when it is answered by another roar behind you. Trapped! Then they come at you from both directions—creatures similar to the ones that tried to drive you off of the cliff. Except that these creatures are without eyes.

But in the narrow tunnel they don't need eyes to find you and tear you limb from limb.

THE END

If you don't like this ending, go back to page 70 and try again.

You try to find your way through the confusing passageways of the witch's maze. A faint, eerie glow in the tunnels gives you just enough light to see where you are going. But you don't seem to be going *anyplace.*

Finally, you see a bright glow up ahead. You are all so excited that you dash toward it. When you get there, though, you are not sure it's where you want to be. You are in a wide, open space surrounded by huge rocks carved in the shape of giant skulls. In the center is a bonfire surrounded by incredibly ugly witches. They all turn to look at you with blazing, hypnotic eyes. You are suddenly paralyzed—you can't move a muscle. Warkus with his own magic powers manages to put up more of a fight. He hurls something at the witches and one of them bursts into flame, sinking to the ground screaming. But there are too many of them for him, and soon he, like the rest of you looks like a frozen statue.

"Sooo, you've all arrived just in time for our little ceremony, have you," says one of the witches, cackling.

Then you are seized by a force that makes you move against your will. One by one you all walk into the flames.

THE END

If you don't like this ending, go back to page 78 and try again.

Carefully, you work your way along the maze of paths that go up the side of the mountain. The trail gets steeper and steeper. Soon you are pulling yourself hand over hand over the rocks. You almost slip a few times as a rock comes loose under your foot and goes bouncing down the side, sometimes starting a landslide.

You are about halfway up the mountain when you hear a deep, rumbling sound above you. You look up in horror as tons of rock come roaring down on top of you.

THE END

If you don't like this ending, go back to page 82 and try again.

You search up and down the castle corridors for the throne room.

"This looks like it could be it," Thea says.

"It's definitely a large room," Teppin says. "It can't hurt to take a look"

A large bronze door leads into the room. Inside it is too dark for you to see where you are. As your eyes get used to the darkness you stare in horror at rows and rows of sleeping creatures, hideous monsters for the most part. You've stumbled into the room where Kralux has his castle guards temporarily in a deep sleep.

"Let's get out of here fast," says Warkus. "I don't want to be here when these creatures wake up."

But they are already waking. Going through the door to the room triggered a mechanism set to revive them. As you rush toward the door, several of the creatures spring into action and bar your escape. Those you might be able to handle—but not the two dozen of them charging you from behind.

THE END

If you don't like this ending, go back to page 86 and try again.

"This is the weirdest thing I've ever been in," Teppin says. "Everything is spinning around. I'm getting dizzy."

"This whole maze must be floating up into the air," Thea says. "Every once in a while I catch a glimpse through the floor of the ground far below. Then the floor becomes opaque again."

"I see it too," you say. "In fact, the walls seem to be dissolving. We're up in the clouds."

"I hope we can get safely back down to the ground when this illusion vanishes," Thea says.

An evil laugh echoes through what is left of the illusion maze. It's Zinkor. "Ha!" he sneers. "You'll get back down all right, but unless you can fly like birds, you're going to have a hard landing—a *very* hard landing.

Suddenly, you find yourselves falling through the air. The maze has vanished. You can see the figures of the guardsmen far below, looking like small, black dots.

I sure hope that young wizard can save us, you think to yourself as you plummet downward like a stone falling from the sky. But he can't.

THE END

If you don't like this ending, go back to page 34 and try again.

You climb higher and higher up into the mountains. After a while, you see the tall cone of the fiery mountain directly above you. The smoke from it fills the sky. Now and then, you feel the mountain shake. Also the trail under your feet is beginning to get warm. You can feel the heat right through the soles of your boots.

Then suddenly, there is an explosion, and a stream of molten rock comes pouring out of a large fissure in the side of the mountain behind you.

Then, a brilliantly glowing fountain of lava bursts forth in front of you. You are all trapped between the two of them.

You are all trying to go sideways, when the rock opens up beneath your feet and you fall headlong into a flaming pool of molten rock.

THE END

If you don't like this ending, go back to page 82 and try again.

The walls of the witch's maze glow with a faint light.

"This maze is endless!" exclaims Teppin.

"Don't give up," Warkus says. "I sense an exit of some sort just around the next bend in the tunnel."

"You do! Then let's get out of here!" Thea exclaims, rushing forward.

"Don't go so fast!" Warkus warns. "There still may be dangers there."

"Whatever they are, I'll take care of them," says Teppin drawing his long knife.

"Unfortunately, there are many dangers that you can't defend yourself against with a knife," says Warkus.

Their talk is cut short by a sudden and total darkness. An ice-cold wind blows past. A ring of ghostly forms appears around you.

"You've come to join our demonic circle and become witches yourselves," an eerie unseen voice says.

"Never!" Warkus screams.

"We shall see, we shall see," the voice says in a rising pitch that ends in a high note that seems to ring through your head. Suddenly, your mind is reeling. You hear a voice saying, "I pledge myself to evil and the devil himself."

Go to next page.

Then you realize that it is your own voice. What are you saying? You can't be doing it. But you no longer have any choice.

THE END

If you don't like this ending, go back to page 78 and try again.

The dungeons are dark and slimy with water dripping from the high ceilings. The floor itself is slippery. You search down one corridor after another, but you can't find Kralux's hiding place. As you pass through one of the many dungeon rooms, the pressure of your weight on the floor triggers one of Kralux's diabolical mechanisms. Heavy doors on both sides of the room slam shut, trapping you inside. Walls on opposite sides of the room start to rumble and move toward you. When they meet in the middle, you will be crushed.

"Can you do anything!" you ask Warkus desperately.

'I can't," Warkus says, a look of fear on his face. "Kralux has magic-proofed this room with a spell. It would take me days to decipher it and work out a counter spell. And we don't have that much time."

And that's true. All you can do is stand there watching as the walls come together.

THE END

If you don't like this ending, go back to page 92 and try again.

You all work your way through the underground maze. Warkus leads, shining the light from Zinkor's rod far ahead into the darkness so that you can see where you are going. Thea and Teppin follow after him. You you are behind *them*.

Suddenly, Warkus lets out a shout and vanishes, light and all. Thea and Teppin are also shouting, but you can't make out what they are saying. They seem to be rushing away from you. You dash ahead. Then, without warning, you find yourself sliding down a long, slippery ramp in the dark. Seconds later, you sail over an edge and into space. After a long drop, you hit the surface of a body of water.

You have all plunged into a deep underground pool. You swim over to the walls. They are smooth and slippery. You are trapped. Warkus it turns out didn't know how to swim and sank like a rock. Not that being able to swim will do *you* much good. You can tread water for only so long.

THE END

If you don't like this ending, turn to page 98 and try again.